Éphraïm Mikhaël

HALYARTES

AND OTHER POEMS IN PROSE

Translated and with an Introduction by
Brian Stableford

HALYARTES

EPHRAÏM MIKHAËL was the form of his name adopted by Georges Michel, who attended Mallarmé's *mardis*, and started a splinter group of his own, "Les Moineaux francs" [The House-Sparrows] in collaboration with his friend Bernard Lazare, whose members included Pierre Quillard and Saint-Pol-Roux. He published a small collection of poems, *L'Automne* in 1886 and wrote three plays, one in collaboration with Lazare and one with Catulle Mendès, before dying young of tuberculosis.

BRIAN STABLEFORD has been publishing fiction and non-fiction for fifty years. His fiction includes an eighteen-volume series of "tales of the biotech revolution" and a series of half a dozen metaphysical fantasies set in Paris in the 1840s, featuring Edgar Poe's Auguste Dupin. His most recent non-fiction projects are *New Atlantis: A Narrative History of British Scientific Romance* (Wildside Press, 2016) and *The Plurality of Imaginary Worlds: The Evolution of French* roman scientifique (Black Coat Press, 2016); in association with the latter he has translated approximately a hundred and fifty volumes of texts not previously available in English, similarly issued by Black Coat Press.

CONTENTS

INTRODUCTION

GEORGES ÉPHRAÏM MICHEL, who signed his literary works Éphraïm Mikhaël, was born in Toulouse on 25 June 1866. Having studied for some years at the Lycée de Toulouse, he went to Paris in 1881 to complete his education at the Lycée Condorcet and the Sorbonne, and then obtained employment at the Bibliothèque Nationale. His early poems were collected in *L'Automne* (1886), which became one of the important exemplars of the burgeoning Symbolist Movement.

Mikhaël persuaded a correspondent from his southern homeland who shared his literary interests with great enthusiasm, Lazare Bernard—whose signed his published works Bernard Lazare—to come to Paris in 1886, and the two became the core members of a group of young poets who all attended Stéphane Mallarmé's salon, and it was under the influence of Mallarmé's literary theories that Mikhaël became a forceful member of the Symbolist Movement. The group adopted the name Les Moineaux Francs [the House-Sparrows]; the other members were Rodolphe Darzens, Pierre Quillard, Paul Pierre Roux (who signed his published work Saint-Pol-Roux) and René Ghil, all of whom became ardent propagandists for Symbolism as well as significant exemplary practitioners, in prose as well as verse, helping to carry forward the tradition of prose poetry developed by Charles Baudelaire and continued by Mallarmé.

In collaboration with Bernard Lazare, Mikhaël wrote a drama based on a short story by J. W. Goethe, *La Fiancée de Corinthe* (1888). He wrote the libretto for a lyrical *féerie* [magical play], *Le Cor fleuri* [The Flowery Horn], with music by the teenage Fernand Halphen, then reckoned something of a prodigy, which was staged at the Théâtre Libre in the same year; a different version, with new material supplied to the libretto by another of Mallarmé's disciples, André-Ferdinand Hérold, was performed at the Opéra-Comique in 1904.

In association with Catulle Mendès, Mikhaël also wrote one act of the libretto for a lyrical drama, *Briséis*—the first of a projected three, based on the same Goethe story as *La Fiancée de Corinthe*—with music by Emmanuel Chabrier, who was the initiator of the project; he and Mendès presumably recruited Mikhaël's assistance because of his work on the previous adaptation of the story; they were unable to complete the project before Mikhaël's untimely death from tuberculosis on 5 May 1890, by which time Chabrier was also in very poor health; the latter did not live to see the existing fragment produced, in 1899.

The author's friends were quick to assemble a definitive collection of *Oeuvres de Éphraïm Mikhaël*, which was published posthumously by Alphonse Lemerre in 1890, adding a good deal of new verse material to the poetry reprinted from *L'Automne*, as well as assembling the poems in prose to which Mikhaël had paid particular attention. One of the friends who helped in the compilation of the volume, Stuart Merrill, an American resident in Paris ardently affiliated to the Symbolist school, was quick to translate some of the prose poems collected therein for use in his showcase anthology of *Poems in Prose* (1890). The most substantial of the others, "Halyartès," which had previously appeared in the August 1889 issue of *La Grande Revue de Paris et de Saint-Petersbourg*, was swiftly reprinted in *La Vie Populaire*, the literary supplement to the Parisian newspaper with the largest circulation, *Le Petit Parisien*.

The *Oeuvres* also includes a number of prose fragments, the commencements of long stories, perhaps even of novels, but it did not seem to me to be appropriate to pad out the present volume, thin as it is, with unfinished works. The works translated here only give a foretaste of the work the author might have gone on to do, but it is mature work, and its spectrum offers a reasonably comprehensive account of the author's literary ambitions and philosophical attitude—the latter inevitably colored by the disease that, as he was all too well aware, was gradually killing him.

These translations were made from the copy of *Oeuvres de Éphraïm Mikhaël* reproduced on the Bibilothèque Nationale's *gallica* website. Two items are untitled in that collection, having not been titled in manuscript; I have taken the liberty of adding the titles "Trees" and "The Market."

—Brian Stableford

HALYARTES

AND OTHER POEMS IN PROSE

THE TOY SHOP

I DO not recall, at present, either the time or the place, or whether it was a dream. Men and women were going back and forth on a long, sad promenade; I was going back and forth in the crowd, a rich crowd from which the perfume of women rose. And in spite of the mild splendor of furs and velvets that brushed me, in spite of the red smiles of fresh lips glimpsed under delicate veils, a vague ennui gripped me on seeing the monotonous strollers file past like that, to my right and my left.

On a bench, a man was looking at the crowd with strange eyes, and as I approached him I heard him sobbing. Then I asked him what he had to lament thus, and, raising his large feverish eyes toward me, the man who was weeping said: "I'm sad, you see, because I've been locked up here for many days in this toy shop. For many days and many years I've only seen puppets, and I'm tired of being the only living being. They're made of wood, but so marvelously fashioned that they move and talk like me. However, I know that they can only ever make the same movements and only ever say the same things.

"Those beautiful dolls, clad in velvet and furs, which leave behind them, trailing in the air, an enamoring odor of iris, are even better articulated. Their mechanisms are even more delicate than the others, and when one knows how to activate them, one has the illusion of life."

He fell silent for a moment; then, with the grave voice of those who remember, he said: "Once, I had taken one, delightfully frail, and I often held it in my arms in the evening. I had said so many very tender things to it that I had ended up believing that it understood them; and I had tried so hard to warm it up with kisses that I believed it to be alive. But I saw clearly, afterwards, that it too, like the others, was a doll full of bran.

"For a long time I hoped that one of the puppets might make a novel gesture, or pronounce a word that the others hadn't already said. Now, I'm weary of whispering my dreams to them. I'm bored, and I'd like to get out of this toy shop in which I've been locked. I beg you, if you can, take me outside, outside, where the living brings are . . ."

THE WAKE

ON THE JASPER of the lake, an ebony junk with black sails, which is sailing without oarsmen, opens a long snowy wake. It is toward the Occident that it is going, slowly—oh, so slowly that one can scarcely hear the frisson of its sad wings. And yet, in the calm languor of the evening, I can now perceive an immaterial sound that is a cry exhaled by the soul of the junk.

The soul of the junk is moaning, and in that strange moan my mind recognizes—as the senses can separate two mingled odors—ennui and fear; because the junk, for hours, has wearied of seeing that wake, the color of shrouds, behind it. It would like to flee from it, in order to go and repose out there, near the magic palaces of red copper built by the setting sun, or stop silently, in order that the lake around it will no longer be anything but a plain of green marble.

But an imperious wind incessantly inflates its sails, and it hollows out itself, with its heavy keel, the wake that wearies and frightens it.

Then a voice, so mysterious and so intimate that I do not know whether it is coming from the junk or my soul, murmurs in the violet evening air: "Oh, no longer to see behind me, on the lake of Eternity, the implacable wake of Time!"

ROYALTY

WHEN the sword was placed in his hand and the crown with ten gold fleurons on his head, and when heralds clad in red dalmatics cried his name to the people, the Prince was saddened. In the pride of his new royalty he retained the thought that innumerable generations of kings had received the crown and the sword before him. As a young child he had dreamed of unknown joys and inviolate glories, but now the banal mantle of sovereigns was being thrown over his shoulders.

He reigned over his people. Armies covered in iron won battles for him, and he knew that his memory would shine in the future like the blaze of a conflagration. However, he was afflicted because his thoughts resembled the thoughts of other men, and they only came to perch in his mind as unfamiliar wood-pigeons haunt all dovecots. And as he had heard monks proclaiming the vanity of joys, he thought: *Dolor alone is infinite. I will have a dolor greater than human dolors, a dolor that no one has known before.*

Then he had the clarions of his men-at-arms sounded throughout the city, and in the public square a scaffold hung with black velvet was erected. When the people had assembled, the executioner's assistants, clad in bloody tunics, led the King's young friend to the scaffold, his best-beloved friend. She wept and appealed to her Lord, and she was so beautiful in her divine despair that she felt that she was adored momentarily by thousands of men. But the King appeared in the public square and climbed the steps of the scaffold in his mantle the color of the sky, on which golden embroideries made the flight of heraldic eagles resplendent. Implacable and silent, he knelt the dear condemned down on the velvet and, taking the ax of punishment in his royal hand, he cut off the beloved head with a single stroke.

Every day and every night, in the Oratory of the Palace, his forehead on the steps of the altar, he implored the Queen of Angels: "Our Lady of the Afflicted, enable my dolor to be visible, as your heart pierced by the seven mystic swords is visible in your images. And that will be the sign of expiation."

The Virgin heard him.

He traveled the countries of the earth, and everywhere in his passage the trees took on the colors of autumn. The bells of churches sounded the knell of their own accord, and the walls of cities dressed in mourning. And that was not a vain funeral din, but every stroke of the bell and every funereal color corresponded to a sad thought in the soul of the King. It was his dolor, transparent in accordance with his wish, and, having become material, it filled the world.

But he was as proud as a god in suffering as no other had suffered, and he marched in the glory of his mourning, as dismal and splendid as a black sun.

While he went thus, making night and winter everywhere he passed, he arrived in a great plain bordered by rigid trees. There, twelve old men were sitting in a circle, immobile on their seats of stone and as mute as the statues that guard tombs.

The King advanced toward them and cried to them in a loud voice: "Look at me, old men, in order that you may see before dying the man who has known a new dolor."

But the old men got up all together, uttering loud cries, and one of them replied to the King: "Man, do not boast before us of feeling what no one has felt before, for we are the Months of the Year, and the Master has established us in order to punish those who have disdained the happiness of crowds. Since you have sinned by virtue of pride, you will not be liberated from Life; but, tortured by the ineffable shame of being ignorant of the unknown, you will remain our prisoner until the end of time, the prisoner of the Months of the Year."

Then, while the buccinas of the archangels resounded in the distant heavens, the King felt his crown fall and his will die, and he entered into the circle of the twelve eternal Jailers.

THE CAPTIVE

I DO NOT KNOW for what superb and inexpiable sin the cold princess is captive in the hall with copper walls. Immobile, and as if proudly flattered by the gaze of invisible crowds, sitting on a throne between two golden chimeras, she is languid, and is doubtless contemplating her insolent beauty in the mirrors on the walls.

However, she is getting up now, and, her eyes still ardent with dreams that the day before has not expelled, she walks toward the metallic walls. In their transparency she sees, as if in luminous dawn mist, a vague form coming toward her, the voluptuous form of a woman with scattered hair. Quivering with supernatural amour, murmuring words of welcome, she runs toward the royal vision, opening her arms. But she has recognized her own splendor, and her nostrils scent in the hall the unique perfume of her flesh. Then, sad and weary, in her unfastened crimson robe, she returns to sit down and weep between the ironic chimeras.

"Me," she says. "Me again!"

Around her, the hall raises its implacable polished walls: no friendly florets or ancient weapons; everywhere, reflected by the copper, the captive alone ornaments her prison.

For many hours she has been suffering ennui, the cold princess guarded by her image. Now she hates herself; now she would like to cover with veils the great mirrors that are her eternal jailer. However, a window is open; if she could see through that window the wandering grape-gatherers in the vines, or the harvesters plunging their arms into the fleece of the wheat-fields, or only—even that would be divine—the grave oxen hollowing out black furrows in the crepuscular plain! How recklessly she would lean out of her window, and how she would blow long fraternal kisses to the fields in labor.

Alas, the road that passes down below is perpetually deserted; it has neither a beginning nor an end, and the black trees that border it have the solemn rumble of waters flowing toward the Ocean. In her dolor, the princess rips her garments; her necklaces, torn away, spill their gems with a mocking rattle, and beneath the tatters of her lacerated crimson attire, she appears entirely in the mirrors, which exalt in the futile glory of her rich nobility.

In the end, however, the door is about to open. If only it were the hour of forgiveness! If only the handsome conqueror clad in light were going to enter! If only some infatuated voice were going to cry: "I have come to liberate you from yourself!"

No, it is a slave, who offers rare fruits and precious wines in emerald cups. And that slave also wears crimson garments; she too allows the heavy treasure of her tresses stream to the floor, and, bodily and facially, she is—more so than a sister-similar to the princess. In addition, she is good and gentle, and speaks a hoarse Oriental language, which makes words of amity resemble the gasps of a dove.

But in the beauty of the envoy, the princess only rediscovers her own beauty, and the consoling words only make her think of her own voice. And that is why the dolorous princess expels angrily the beautiful loving slave, crueler than the mirrors.

MIRACLES

I T is in an ancient and rich city on the shore of a cerulean ocean, in a strange city where, among the obelisks and the pylons, machines swarm and rumble. From the height of a long marble terrace the poet Azahel contemplates a hive of ambitious sails in the harbor. In the fortunate dusk, under a sky vibrant with flocks of swallows, he is thinking about the futility of the hours.

But he is aware that in this city, where scholars and sages and doctors of law live, he alone knows the infirmity of reason, and he thinks about the men who bear ridiculous common sense through the ages, like a precious and heavy reliquary, and because he has disdained it, he glorifies himself in his heart.

Now, amid the crowd in the port, a stranger appears clad in a woolen mantle of a noble and obsolete form. His eyes, like antique gems, seem to retain memories of primordial visions, and beneath his feet the paving stones quiver respectfully.

At the moment when the poet Azahel has descended into the crowd, the stranger has raised his arm toward the sky, and now he cries, with a voice that resonates like the clarions of temples: "Men, I am a prophet of God. I have come to enable you to hear the Word, and those who want to follow me, I shall lead away, walking over the waves of the sea, into the veritable Promised Land."

Then a rumor of disappointment rose up in the crowd. Young men, after having gazed alternately at the prophet and the sky, where the vesperal mist is thickening, leave at a negligent pace. Scholars observe silently, and merchants, having darted a last glance at their good vessels at anchor in the peaceful harbor, move away shrugging their shoulders. One doctor of law, however, has said with a smile: "Master, if you are the envoy of God, show us a sign. In truth, can you not, in accordance with the rite of prophets, cure the mute and the blind?"

There was one blind man and one mute in the port. The prophet imposed his hands on their foreheads, and the blind man opened his eyes, and the mute spoke in a clear voice.

The prophet asked: "Is that a sufficient sign, and would you like to follow me?"

But the crowd remains immobile, the blind man shakes his head and the mute cries: "I don't believe you!"

That is why the stranger extends his confident right hand toward the horizon, now full of night, and repeats the sacred words of *Genesis*: "Let there be light!"

And a spring-like dawn bursts forth in the Orient.

Anxiously, the doctors of law draw nearer to the scholars. However, not one person advances toward the sea.

Then, with the sadness of a vanquished angel, the tall stranger goes to sit down pensively on the steps of an ancient temple, before the doors, which have been closed for thousands of years. Gradually, the crowd disperses; the scholars and the doctors desert the port, and as they return from there they feel less troubled, because the natural night has returned.

Only Azahel has remained near the closed temple, and he contemplates the man from the beyond. What if he were truly the Envoy? Oh, to recognize him, to greet him, to follow him to the land of election! But Azahel's mind is obscured by terrestrial ideas, and he is only able to think that the man is very handsome because of his tall stature and his godlike gaze.

Suddenly, the old man stands up and walks toward the poet. "Azahel, you loved a virgin who is dead. I will return her to you."

Immediately, clad in a shroud and emerging rosy from death like the freshness of a matinal sea, a young woman appears. Laughing and forgetful of the divine things of the tomb, she extends her arms toward the beloved.

But he flees in terror through the silent streets; amid the pylons and the obelisks and the simulacra of forgotten gods; he flees, obfuscated by the miracle, like a nocturnal bird frightened by torchlight. And it is only when he has returned to the peaceful marble terrace that he dares to turn his gaze toward the port haunted by prodigies.

At that moment a mysterious light is shining in the direction of the Orient. Over the smooth ocean, the tall Biblical old man is passing tranquilly, and the reflection of stars in the water makes a double border of diamonds for his route.

Now Azahel would like to get up and also go away over the miraculous waves. But he senses that he is so heavy with reason that he cannot even raise his shameful hands toward the Envoy who is going away.

THE EVOCATION

AS the conqueror's army emerged from the forest, the barbarian archers of the advance guard shouted that they could see an immense and bizarre city in the distance. Out there, in the russet mists of the Occident, rose high marble towers, and the blood of the evening fell as if from sacred patens over terraces paved with gold.

But when the army had drawn closer, it was recognized that the city was—and doubtless had been for centuries—silent and deserted. Then the soldiers, lowering their pikes, entered peacefully, and marched for a long time along solemn streets, past overgrown walls and closed doors.

In the end, in a square in front of a colossal temple, an old man advanced. "Strangers," he said, "you have come into an austere place. If you are impure and avid, go away toward the sumptuous cities of Asia. You will find no treasures here to pillage, nor any virgins to violate. Go away, for this is the city of the gods. However, if you retain here, warriors from fortunate lands, some care for the distant heavens, come toward the lamps that no terrestrial wind can extinguish, into the sanctuary where, like an august captive lion, the Divinity consents to the gazes of human beings."

The soldiers, weary and surprised, murmured. However, because of the long marches they had accomplished, they decided to spend the night beside fires lit in the supernatural city. But they could not sleep, because the thought of the imminent god troubled them.

That is why, little by little, the temple filed up with an insolent crowd awaiting the divine vision. There were men there of every sort: imperious soldiers, timid valets of the army, ironic scribes and a sage from the banks of the Ganges emaciated by frightful fasts and dispossessed by eternal alms, whom the conqueror kept in his retinue for the sake of vanity.

When daylight appeared, all those men emerged from the temple, shivering for having meditated, and in the square they questioned one another, anxiously. Some had seen strange faces, grimacing and cruel, partly veiled by bloody fogs; others announced grotesque gods with enormous bellies and stupid joyous faces. Some also spoke of a smiling god who designated the world with his hand and then agitated his arm as if by way of apology.

But the silent sage went back into the temple and asked the old man: "Why, then, exhibitor of gods, have you not given all these men the same vision? I watched with them, and amid the music of paradise, I saw an ineffable aurora of splendor and benevolence blossom and grow. Why, then, have you lied to them? Why have my brothers in the army not known the dream of God?"

"Stranger, you have all seen the God. Do you not know that the heavens, perhaps dreams and liars, are only a great mirror in which everyone sees himself clad in eternity? They have seen themselves in the sky and they are blaspheming. Listen to what they are saying."

Then the sage looked out through a window. Irritated by those ridiculous and bloody gods, the crowd was bringing torches in order to burn the temple, and rushed upon it with laughter and insults.

Then, for the ears of the sage, the proffered syllables became resplendent with unusual meaning, and in a marvelous primitive language that had suddenly become intelligible, he heard the blasphemers confess their sins and their crimes, and proclaim before the holy doors their own negligibility.

TREES

FROM the platform of the tram I watch the black trees flee. The sky is a profound gray. One imagines that it has always been thus. The trees are stiff and slender, spreading out in infinitely meager and sad branches. At the far end of the avenue, the last two trees, the most distant that I can perceive, seem to be vaporized, dissolved marvelously in the air. One might think them spectral trees, forms of trees made entirely of mist.

Those two are fading away, blurring, losing themselves in the great gray beyond. Others appear to me thus; and I have the dream, for a brief moment, that the sky is swallowing those phantom trees, one by one.

THE MARKET

AT the corner of the Boulevard de Clichy there is an open air market. It is cold; no bright, beautiful fruits, nothing but dull, gray, wretched things, fish and sad herbs. I like to traverse that crowd. One encounters strange and sinister figures there. The women who are selling things, old, enormous and corpulent, are rather grotesque. But there are dolorous old men who offer their merchandise with so much sadness; their complexions are earthen and bleak; their wrinkles seem to be suffering; and their unquiet, misty eyes are bloody, as if wounded. One, especially, is small and thin, with an unkempt beard compressed by a red handkerchief supporting a sick jaw. A nasty humility curbs him; he must be wicked, but he seems so frightened! He offers salad vegetables with a fearful, tragic gesture; one might think that he is presenting expiatory sheaves before him, vaguely, in order to ward off scattered evil spells.

HALYARTES

THE MAGI are assembling tonight on the Funeral Mountain, near the sacred gulf into which the warriors, to the salute of tympani and buccinas, throw royal coffins. The day before, in the capital of Bactriana, an army in mourning returned, bringing back the body of the king on a splendid and sinister ebony chariot. The funerary rites having been accomplished, the corpse had been wrapped in a shroud sewn by the virgin princesses, and in the evening, at the moment when the sun fell toward the lakes where the first Magus purified himself, the captains and the masters of the cavalry, having climbed up the mountain paths, had thrown the coffin into the gulf, as was prescribed.

Now, in the villages and in the plains, huge lugubrious pyres were blazing; cavaliers wearing cilices were on watch on the roads; at intervals, heralds clamored a signal. And clarions called continually into the darkness, for no one, because of the immense mourning, ought to sleep that night.

On the mountain, the Magi deliberated. Anxiously, they showed one another, among the stars whose names they knew, an unusual constellation. A great rumor of affliction rose up. The youngest of the Magi, with cries of interrogation and gestures of prayer, pressed tumultuously around the initiator, Halyartes of Ecbatana. Sure of his science and doubtless disdainful of future glimpses, he smiled placidly at the bright fateful night.

He consented to respond, however. He spoke in a grave and seemingly distant vice. "Sons," he said, "the watchers who signaled these menacing ambulant stars were wrong to groan; there will be no misfortune."

Then cries burst forth, more suppliant. Breathless with hope, the Magi hastened toward the initiator. Some extended their hands as if a salutary alms were about to come to them. They cried: "Speak! Speak, quickly!"

Halyartes said: "Certainly, you have interpreted the signs well; these stars do, indeed, signify that a danger might emerge for us from the child that the priests will invest this morning with the paternal purple. Without a doubt, if he were to grow up and prosper, King Pherohil, in one evening of his old age, would annihilate the entire race of Magi and will throw our sacred books into the flames. And the earth would then be tenebrous, because no one any longer would be able to see the legible signs traced by the stars, and the voices of the night would speak in vain in the definitive silence in which humans would sleep, deaf henceforth. Yes, all that would be accomplished in the old age of King Pherohil. But can I not ensure, myself, that a mortal dies young?"

As he spoke those words, Halyartes turned toward the plains, and he darted cold, cruel glances in the direction of the royal terraces, where, in a luminous mist, great elevated beacons were raising their flames of mourning.

Then a young man wearing the white linen robe in which recent initiates were clad cried, impatiently: "Master! Master! Have you not looked at the sky, then? See! Do the stars not proclaim the inevitable triumph of Pherohil? You can see clearly that he cannot die young. If foreigners come to attack him, armored with iron and helmed with steel, their armor will shatter of its own accord at the slightest touch of his lance, like defective robes; and the bucklers of Sogdiana, made from an enormous warrior diamond, will be nothing more, if he strikes them with his sword, than futile jewels. If the breath of the plague blows over him, it will pass by, as suave and salutary as a breeze bringing the petals of benevolent flowers. In sum, as you know, it is written in the Occidental sky, in the direction of Chaldea, that no assassin's dagger can be raised against Pherohil. Is he not of the sacred race? Does not an occult power of the gods protect his family? No one, even one of us, would dare to kill him. And even you, Master, if it required a murder to save the ancient science of the Magi, and the Books, and the things of the heavens, would you strike the king?"

Placidly, Halyartes replied: "No! The gods forbid it. But what does it matter?" he added. "Since the death of the king is necessary to us, he will die. Battles will be fortunate for him. Plagues will spare him. Tigers will lick his feet. No murderer, not even me, will find a dagger or a philter for him. So be it! Know, however, that he will be full of youthful strength when his hour comes. Long before the time when he would accomplish the prophecies, you, the Magi, will see him, liberated from deadly stars, descend into the shadow that is here."

And the initiator, with an ample gesture, as if swearing an oath, indicated the gulf where coffins were thrown.

✳

36

When the week of mourning had ended, the princes of the army and the twelve priests of the grand temple decided that the royal child would be confided to the care of Halyartes. Henceforth, when he walked in the palace gardens, the flag-decked streets of the city or in the country roads, Pherohil always had the initiator beside him, mysterious and grave in his white robe. In a matter of days, Halyartes had tamed the wild little king, who followed him as meekly as a charmed lion.

The child turned continually toward the Magus as if to await his thoughts; it seemed that only the spirit of the master animated Pherohil. Jealously, Halyartes kept away the servants and the servants' children; he created an austere and marvelous solitude around his disciple. Always alone, they walked, talking about celestial sciences amid the prodigies of the garden; alone they climbed into the gilded boat drawn by submissive swans; and they were alone when they went to wander, as a game, in the Orchard-of-Treasures, planted long ago by the king's ancestors, the orchard where a durable dew of pearls trembled on the silver branches.

What the master said during these excursions, no one knew. Only the women of the palace remarked that Pherohil no longer laughed gloriously like other children. Sometimes, in the good quietude of the evening, Halyartes and Pherohil sat on a marble perron. The hour was mild; the pigeons and the peacocks searched for seeds among the scattered gems; the tame gazelles that wandered over the blue grass of the lawns seemed to be grazing on the light.

Then the Magus read powerful words in a book that came from far away, and the child sighed, delectably sad, and extended his hands toward the shadow, as if he were caressing the dusk.

Years went by. The day came when the falconers and the hunters brought Pherohil, now of an age to hunt, the royal bow. Very robust, the young king launched sure arrows that plunged profoundly into cedar-wood stakes. To exercise him in killing, sparrow-hawks and gerfalcons were released into the air, but he allowed the predatory birds to fly away, and threw down his bow silently.

As slaves pursued the flying gerfalcons with arrows, the king returned to the palace, and that evening, in spite of the clowns and the mimes, he refused to smile. Pherohil left the feast before it was finished. As he was no longer able to keep a secret for long he took the Magus with him, and they were heard talking for a long time in a murmur of sad confidences. Then a flame of joy was seen in Halyartes' eyes, and during the night the watchmen guarding the terrace perceived the initiator raising a clay lamp toward the sky in a sign of thanks.

From that day on, often, in the crepuscular hours, Halyartes took his disciple into the Beggars' quarter. There, in the fetid back-streets, amid the filth of the gutters, swarmed a population of the infirm, the mutilated and the leprous. A hideous sick crowd surrounded Pherohil. Dwarfs dragged themselves to his knees; children devoid of feet crawled before him. Wounds, ulcers and pustules were displayed with a species of ironic pride; mutes grunted mysteriously; the blind lamented from the depths of their great familiar darkness. Deformed hands were extended; hairy fingers gabbed the fringes of the royal robe. In houses with open doors, on polluted and bloody beds, hateful and furious bedridden women howled like wounded beasts. Old men, too feeble to descend into the street, stuck their spectral faces to the windows. Suppliant monsters surged forth everywhere, which seemed to have lifted themselves out of the coffin, and men yelled with black mouths, as if they had already bitten the tumulary earth.

The king went by, saying consolatory words, throwing handfuls of gold. Sometimes, sickened, oppressed by an ineffable malaise, he wanted to flee from the horrible streets; but the inflexible Magus brought him back, guided him and forced him to see. In any case, the beggars followed him now. They came from all the Bactrian villages, for Pherohil's renown had spread; he was proclaimed to be very good and very merciful, and poets sang his praises to the sound of hieratic harps and flutes.

However, the king became sad. Sometimes, amid the splendors of the palace, he had a proud smile again; but Halyartes approached, and the king immediately became somber, as if a divine shadow had passed over him.

The courtiers interrogated one another. What secret trouble was tormenting the king? It was sometimes said that he felt remorse, but what remorse was possible in that marvelous soul? No repentance could trouble that king, who pardoned murderers, divested himself of his sacred purple for the poor and prayed to the gods for his enemies. Everything that gives men joy, however, rendered him strangely pensive, and on the day when his captains announced a victory, amid the din of triumphant clarions, resplendent standards and glittering weapons, he hid his face in his hands and sobbed before the happy crowd.

In order to distract him from his strange malaise, mention was made to him of a distant princess of India, whose supernatural beauty was attested by voyagers. Out there, it was said, toward the land of the five rivers, people named the Queen of Srinagar in a long rumor of admiration. Conquerors had come, offering gems and unknown flowers, spreading rare perfumes at the feet of the implored queen; but she, haughtily distracted, struck them all with the golden lotus that was her scepter. There was such a power to be loved in her that the grimmest individuals, thinking of the insult received, smiled gently as if at the memory of caresses.

Often, she went out on foot, all alone, in the streets of her capital. Confidently, she traversed the respectful crowds of males quivering with futile desire. The young men watched her pass by with a voluptuous despair, so glacial and white that she seemed to be guarded by a magical polar mist. And the tenebrous perfume that her flesh exhaled was so powerful that even women dared not hate her. Even wives scorned because of her and mothers whose sons had died of loving her did not make gestures of malediction as she passed by. Mute and resigned, they contemplated her as voyagers admire the murderous lightning in a stormy sky.

On the advice of Halyartes, Pherohil had a sumptuous retinue prepared and he departed for Srinagar. The king's horse was caparisoned with lace; young slaves sang and danced along the roads, and semi-naked women, with only one shoulder covered by a panther-skin, conducted with golden thyrses great carts in which wildflowers were heaped up on the way.

Pherohil entered Srinagar. Tremulous, tortured by the presentiment of a terrible amour, he went toward the palace. It was the hour when the princess was due to go out, and an anxious crowd was waiting. A great black door opened slowly and the queen appeared. From the top of a porphyry staircase she perceived Pherohil. Immediately, she stopped, and shuddered. Then, slowly, almost hesitantly, she descended the steps and came to abdicate the redoubtable golden lotus at Pherohil's feet. Young men raised their fists toward Pherohil with cries of hatred and suffering; but amid the desperate tumult the two fiancés advanced, divinely elected by one another, their hands united and their lips met victoriously.

Celebrations commenced the next day. In spite of the precious wines springing forth in fountains in the squares and spreading through the fields in disdainful streams; in spite of the sapphires and the chrysoprases that were thrown like seeds into the furrows; and in spite of the tons of gold negligently spilled at crossroads, the young men of Srinagar witnessed the marriage sadly. They loved the queen with such an amour that jealousy turned them away from the fountains of wine, the fields sown with gems and the crossroads cluttered with gold. Morose, they sat down on the threshold of the palace and they no longer thought about anything except that the queen was going to leave.

When she departed, proudly seated in her chariot beside the king she loved, the people accompanied her with long sobs. Stupidly, men wrapped their arms around the necks of the horses drawing the chariot and bit the white manes with furious kisses. Others, seizing the nuptial veil in the wind, embraced it, weeping. Some, in order to respire once more the perfumes emanated by the queen, assailed the chariot; they leaned toward the embalmed robe and remained there, bewildered and fainting, without the whips of the slaves being able to drive them away. Others, their arms open as if for a possessive embrace, threw themselves in front of the cortege. The hard poles garnished with nails struck them on the breast and they fell in the dust, ecstatic and bloody. There were some who lay down in the road and, their eyes turned toward the fugitive, allowed themselves to be crushed and killed voluptuously by the heavy horses. But the most smitten could not resolve to lose the queen. Obstinately, they ran behind her. Stones were thrown at them; they were struck with knotty sticks; greyhounds and mastiffs were unleashed at them; but, bitten and bloody, they kept following.

Pherohil, when he emerged from the palace, went superbly, with his arm around his chosen spouse, his eyes drowned in a supernatural happiness; but gradually, in the lamentable melee of the crowd, he felt his joy weakening. Abruptly paled under Halyartes' fixed stare, he almost forgot his beloved in bleak reveries, and his arm separated, as if ashamed, from his wife's waist.

The conquered queen leaned toward him, and, kissing her husband's lips slowly, she murmured salutary words: "What does it matter, since I love you?"

But the king seemed to be the captive of some black enchantment. Certainly, he had manifested an immense amour by means of a thousand follies, but the more he adored the queen, the more he was wonderstruck by her, and the more he dreamed dolorously about things that no one could divine. The courtiers began to murmur that strange philters had troubled his reason. As if he wanted to flee invisible specters, he cried incessantly, leaning toward the coachmen: "Faster, faster still!"

Already they had emerged from the sad crowds. Almost all of those who had followed the nuptial flight avidly had succumbed. One after another they had fallen by the roadside, motionless.

The Bactrian mountains appeared. Soon, no doubt, they would enter the city by the Festival Gate, and they would no longer even remember the obsessive cortege. The gates would be closed violently, and the last of the young men of Srinagar would perish in the fields, obscurely.

That day, the Magus, quitting the royal chariot, spoke for a long time to the scouts of the advance guard. They listened respectfully, their right hands applied to the shafts of their spears. Then, at a signal from the Magus, they departed again at a gallop.

Doubtless troubled by Halyartes' words, the old scouts went astray. All night long they traveled through sterile gray plains, and in the morning the cortege presented itself at the side of the city where the Beggars' Quarter was huddled. Supplicants abruptly filled the roads. There was a hideous rush outside the gates.

Crying, imploring, challenging and insulting, the beggars launched forth. They pressed together, jostling one another, and luminous thin fists and sticks were seen, raised in the air. Already, a frightful and grotesque battle was commencing between the mutilated and the dying.

But the king stood up, livid, on the seat of the chariot. "No, not this way! Not this way!" he cried.

The cortege turned round. Via the exterior road, along the rampart, it progressed as far as the next gate. That gate was the Gate of the Dead.

Very numerous, as after days of plague, funerary carts were stationed near the gate. The wailing of widows resounded; orphaned children were appealing lamentably; young men in mourning were sobbing the names of wives. Again the king appeared beside the frightened coachmen. Shivering, his voice punctuated by gasps, he stammered: "Go in by another gate!"

The horses had to turn again, and they took a paved and flowery road that led to the Military Gate. On that side of the city the population was rejoicing triumphantly. Fanfares burst forth. In the distance, the proud rumor of a fortunate army was audible, the whinnying of horses and the rattle of bucklers clinking like cups in a warrior dance. At intervals, the commands of captains responded to one another, monotonous and sonorous; and in the far distance, with a noise of mounting waves, the enormous war machines rumbled on their bronze-rimmed wheels.

But that victorious army was bringing back a convoy of prisoners. Shackled by ropes, their shoulders bruised by wooden yokes, the captives were filing painfully, and the cavaliers of the escort were spurring them with their pikes, alarming them with their rearing horses.

Suddenly, the news spread that the king had arrived. Then there was a tempest of joy. The people sang hymns of praise; women cut branches to strew on the road, hastily weaving garlands. The best dressed took off their brocade veils and hung them from trees like festival banners, and the soldiers lowered their pikes charged with severed heads, in a sign of salutation.

Abruptly, a mounted chief was before the king, and in the silence, in a resounding voice, he told the story of an unexpected attack by rebels and their just rout in the woods. His words excited the people. An immense anger rose up against the captives. Men sang the praises of Pherohil, clamoring his name amorously; they leapt between the horses, seized the prisoners and tied them to the gates of the city. Then they delighted in killing them with stones and arrows.

Pherohil ran forward, his hand raised pacifically to order them to show mercy, but he was too late. The last of the captives tottered under the insulting wound of a child. As the arrow had been unleashed at very close range, it traversed the foreigner's breast, nailing his body to the batten of the gate; and the man stayed there, upright, colossal and frightening. In his last convulsions his hands beat the portal; he seemed to be trying to close it forever, as a vengeance, and as Pherohil advanced, the murdered man stiffened toward him, as if to chase him away and curse him.

Then the king stopped, in a desperate lassitude. As if he no longer dared, now, to enter the city, from which dolors erupted on the threshold of every gate, he fled madly toward the fields. But on the roads, amid the stones and the brambles, the young men of Srinagar were still gasping. Those dying men frightened the king like phantoms; he dared not violate the roads that their agony defended. He turned back incessantly, haggard and bewildered, like a deer tracked by packs of dogs.

Suddenly, he threw himself into the only deserted road, the somber road that led to the Funeral Mountain. Panicked courtiers followed him, calling to him, imploring him. He turned round; and, proffering threats for the first time, he cried that he would kill anyone who tried to follow him.

A great tumult of fear had risen at the flight of the king. The people, the soldiers and the members of the cortege mingled and were confused, uttering cries of amazement, and moans, hurling questions, advice and orders at random. Noisily, they surrounded the chariot where the queen lay motionless and cold, as if struck by an invisible arrow.

But when Pherohil had entered beneath the somber branches of the evil road, an anxious silence weighed upon the crowd. The soldiers no longer budged, for fear of rattling their sonorous arms, and the cavalier held their horses religiously. Now, no one could see the king any longer, for the black road had numerous bends, and was lost in the distance behind the woods. But on the horizon, in the full light, great funereal rocks rose up, and the Magus looked in that direction, without impatience and without anguish, as if awaiting an infallible event.

Suddenly, the strange fugitive appeared on the brink of the gulf. Up there, in the solemn splendor of the dusk, Pherohil raised himself up to his full height in his golden robe. Marvelously pale, like a dying god, he climbed the last slopes, and the evening sunlight poured a red light over his tiara like a flood of baptismal blood. For an instant, on the extreme trim of the rocks, Pherohil stopped, and saluted the subject plain with his gaze. Then he made a sad and gentle gesture, the gesture of an exile issuing a benediction as he departs, and he precipitated himself into the sacred gulf.

That evening, again the pyres announcing new funerals blazed on the plains and on the hills. Cavaliers in mourning trod the roads again, and funereal signals responded to one another in the darkness. But beyond the shadow in which the affliction of the people murmured, the Magi delivered themselves to rejoicing on the mountain. The young initiates surrounded Halyartes, pressing him with respectful questions.

"What secret word did you pronounce in order to trouble the king thus?"

"In what divine book did you collect the venomous thoughts that poisoned him?"

"It's said that you know how to evoke the dead; what specter did you summon in order to guide him toward the gulf?"

Halyartes smiled. "Children," he said, "I had no need of enchantments or specters. Simply, with the natural authority of the master over the disciple, I have made that king a monster that the earth could no longer retain."

The initiates were astonished. Halyartes imposed silence on them with an imperious movement of the hand.

"Yes," he went on, "a monster; for the man is a monster to whom the vital air is mortal. I have made Pherohil die of that which makes us live. I was the master of that soul. I poured into it, like the juice of a deadly flower, a terrible goodness. Thanks to me, Pherohil ceased to be a man. I made him better than a man, and that is why he is dead. All the furious passions that surge within us, bite us and tear us apart, I expelled from him. So his heart became sad, like a liberated forest that will suffer forever from there death of wild beasts. Hatred, the red thirst for massacres, envy and the obscure temptation to torture and destroy, were all unknown to him.

"Because I was always present, whispering my will to him continuously, the pallor of inadmissible jealousy and the ardent redness of bestial anger never adhered to his terribly pure visage. He had the sublime and dangerous impotence, the impotence of evil, with the consequence that a formidable enemy was installed in his excessively noble heart. No evil thought could sustain him, or intoxicate him. I had killed his vanity, and even the purple became useless to him, since he could no longer take pride in his legitimate royalty.

"Pitilessly, I forced him to pity. When beggars implored him, he was no longer capable of driving them away from his dream by means of hypocritical consolations. He was no longer able, in feeling compassion for the feeble and the crippled, to rejoice in his own young vigor. But really, profoundly, he felt the woes that he contemplated, and the sovereign, thanks to the deadly gift of pity, descended so far as to be the equal of his supplicants.

"The innumerable dolors of the nation at war tore him apart, and when his armies went on campaign, he it was who suffered from all the long marches, who bled from all the wounds, who agonized in all the death-throes. When a victory was announced to him, he only saw bloody death in assailed cities, and heard above the fanfares the loud maledictions of violated virgins; and all the mourning of the conquered lands entered into his heart.

"The day when he took away the beloved queen, he went mad with pity because of the dolorous lovers who died of his triumph. His amour only served to make him comprehend the sad amour of others, and because he loved recklessly, he suffered recklessly for his rivals. Thanks to my insidious lessons, he could not consent to the cruelty of living, and, knowing that one man's felicity is made of the innumerable misfortunes of distant men, he no longer wanted to reconcile himself to being happy. Such was that king.

"Yesterday, hazard—or, rather, my sagacity and vigilant will—caused all the wounds of the earth to appear before him simultaneously: amour, infirmity, mourning, poverty, defeat, slavery, iniquitous and dishonest massacre. It was too much. That child, whom I cleverly accustomed to bruising himself with the dolor of others, wanted to free himself once and for all from that long torture of loving.

"As you see, I did not employ philters or the formulae of enchantment. It was sufficient for me to render Pherohil slightly different from what we are. Do we, too, not have a word of pity for all the suffering there is on earth? Except that the word in question is vain and deceptive. Pherohil really felt what we all express in confrontation with misfortune. He was good, as you boast of being, but he was sincere, as you only believe yourselves to be. That is why his body was broken voluntarily on the rocks of the mountain."

While the Magus spoke, a soft spring dawn flourished in the sky. Down below, in the fields, a white procession spread out.

Young women carrying golden pitchers on their heads marched between eglantine hedges. Children ran ahead of them, toward the place of sacrifices, of rams with beautiful fleeces. Tall blonde women held in the pleats of their embroidered dresses seeds of wheat and barley, which they threw into the air at every step, with the consequence that wild birds followed them joyfully. Soldiers, devoid of armor and weapons, swung palms and oak branches piously. The voices of priests rose up, chanting prayers:

"Father Sun, fecundator, savior, give us a king as good as Pherohil."

The people, after each verse of the prayer, responded distinctly with the sacramental maxim: "For the wicked are unhappy!"

They all said that in a loud and solemn voice, in accordance with the liturgical rhythm, and the old men inclined their heads, as a sign of intelligence.

THE SOLITARY

Anywhere out of the World[1]

IN ORDER to carry out the orders of a distant king, servants exposed the child in a place of forests and rocks. The abandoned infant was placed on a stone amid monstrous grass; harsh flowers around him opened their hostile red corollas like maws. But that night the jubilee commenced, and the priests gathered in the forest perceived the child.

One of the hierophants, leaning over toward the stone, prophesied. "This one," he said, "is of noble race. He will be delivered from malevolent approaches."

---

1 This epigraph is the title of one of Baudelaire's poems in prose, rendered in English in the original.

The priests sang the customary hymns; then they all went together to confide the child to the king's pastors. A sounder of the conch preceded the procession; they were in mourning and, turning toward the plain, they made tumultuous and desperate plaints resound. But from the depths of the forests the buccina players in white robes responded with rich fanfares and the haughty straight clarions were seen rising in the dawn like golden lilies.

In the shepherds' village the child was named Stellus. He grew up wild and disdainful, and yet, there was a tenebrous tenderness in him. He opened his arms to children. He ran to mothers and hugged them filially. But he suddenly stopped, as if wounded by an unknown evil; he lowered his head and fled toward shadowed corners, toward the broad deserted highways. Other children threw stones at him and beat him with branches; the old men said: "They're right; you ought to play with your brothers."

Meekly, he then tried to follow those of his age when they went into gardens to steal fruit and pillage the beehives. But suddenly, without understanding, he had a desire to weep and to hide.

Often, he fled away from roads and villages, into the forest where he had once been found. A vast peace descended upon him; the friendly branches brushed him with welcome freshness, and it seemed to him that healing hands were being placed on his forehead. Silently, he sat down in a sunlit place, on the edge of a lake so profoundly impregnated with ancient light that it seemed to retain within its shores a marvelous liquid of cinnabar and gold.

Stellus stayed there, without a dream, without desire, intoxicating himself by listening to the wind. At first he heard nothing but a monotonous and confused noise spread over the entire country. Soon, he was able to distinguish the frisson of each wood, of every branch. Then he discerned unusual, supernatural sounds reminiscent of the songs of magical spinners and the sighs of celestial flutes.

And that rumor of the wind had a miraculous power. As he listened to it, Stellus sensed new thoughts surging within him. He understood, he knew and he saw the forest living; he saw the ineffable soul of the trees, the grass and the waters; and sounds fallen from the stars taught him divine things. He was not astonished, however. That revelation only seemed to him to be a recovered memory, and every idea that entered into him was like a returning exile. He listened placidly, and it seemed to him to be quite simple that the information was brought to him by the wind, like flowers plucked from the orchards of the night.

But when the breezes finally fell silent, an immense sadness grew in the child's soul. After the revelatory words that the wind brought him, he felt more prodigiously that he was a stranger. An imperious desire sometimes came to him to repeat to others what he had learned from the forest, but he divined that he would speak in vain, and he remained dolorously silent. When he returned to his companions, a strange malaise oppressed him. Every day he lingered for longer in the forest, in its unexplored sectors. For one entire summer, he lived among the trees. He stayed there, loving and savage, regretting his companions but not daring to return to them. Mist soiled the dusks; a long, sad quivering agitated the branches; the trees leaned backwards, frightened and tremulous, as if baulking fearfully before the approaching winter; the flocks in the short grass grew thin and bleated lamentably at the moon.

A man came from the village to enquire about the belated pastor. Stellus confided his dolor to him; he begged him to leave him in the forest. The man listened with an appearance of understanding. "I can see what you desire," he said, finally. "The priests have told you that you were of a noble race. That doubtless signifies that you are not made to be a herdsman. Go forth into the world in quest of glorious hazards. Be a soldier."

Stellus believed that man. *Yes, he thought, perhaps I will be better among soldiers.*

Having climbed a rock, he saw the troubled fires of a camp in the distance. He left the flocks and followed bitter paths toward battles. The calls of the sentinels on the hills guided his progress; trumpets sounded in the distance, as if to welcome the man that was coming.

His helmet crested by a bronze bird, his armor bristling with nails, Stellus fought with the ax and the sword. He served a conquering king whose army advanced triumphantly, odious to the nations. Such a hatred growled behind the invaders that they killed the wounded in order to spare them the expiatory tortures that the enemy would doubtless have inflicted upon them. And in order that no one would be captured alive, the soldiers were linked together in battle by chains. But a mysterious force pushed Stellus to fight alone.

He tried in vain to get closer to his brothers in arms; and an invisible power moved him away. On nights of alarm, he galloped alone toward perilous positions; he was the solitary torch-bearer who explored the barbaric woods; he was the unique defender of rearguards who was left behind like a martial offering to the gods of war during the flight of kings and captains. And yet, how he would have liked to mingle with his companions, to drink pillaged wine with them in stolen cups, and sing with them around the bivouacs! How he envied those who, on the eve of massacres, slept together fraternally under flapping tents. But he never had companions.

In the days of the first battles he thought: *Doubtless, being of a noble race, I cannot please myself among mercenaries; I would be happy if I were marching with the leaders.* He accomplished such exploits that the kings saluted him as their equal. He received the golden lance and banner and had his place among the princes of the army. But in the ardent cortege of young sovereigns, the ancient dolor surprised him again; in the squares of conquered capitals that he was given as a privilege, he sensed, as in the shepherd village, that he was a passing stranger.

As he was afflicted, an old captain who admired him said to him: "I know what you desire. What you lack, Stellus, is amour. Go forth into the world in quest of some white princess. Be a lover."

Stellus believed the captain. He put ample branches of lilac into his saddle-bag; he rolled vine-branches and foliage around his lance and departed toward amour. Magical birds, dazzling the air with bright wings, fluttered around the cavalier; nuptial perfumes floated over the rivers and fields.

In a land of sunlight and fresh waters, Stellus found the white princess. She was standing beside a spring, drawing water in a silver pitcher; her pale and supple arms were leaning on the rim. The young woman began to laugh because the magical birds settled upon her abruptly, and sprayed bright droplets over her face as they folded their wings. When Stellus approached, she fled.

She ran into the country, and while she ran she laughed. At times she stopped, hastily picked red roses and white roses, and threw them at the cavalier, ironically. Her tawny hair was undone and spread over her shoulders like the mantle of a huntress fabricated from the pelt of a young lioness.

In the end Stellus overtook her, put his arms around her and pulled her up on to his horse. She was still laughing. "Drop the reins," she said. Gently, with caressant words, she guided the tamed charger. She conducted it along a pathway strewn with blue powder to her palace, and that night the sistra and tymbals announced a royal wedding.

The nuptial garlands had not yet faded on the palace balconies when Stellus came to sit down in the gardens, sobbing. He raised his plaintive arms toward the sky and murmured: "Who, then, will come to my aid? Who will advise me?"

Then he saw a tall old sacerdotal man who was listening to him. "Father," said Stellus, "if you are the savior sent to me, if you know hidden things, tell me why I am forever solitary. Tell me why, as a child, I was unable to play with the other children, why I was unable to reveal to young men the words of the wind, nor laugh with the soldiers, nor sleep voluptuously beside my wife?"

And in a supernatural voice, the old man replied: "Stellus, Stellus, since the enchantments of the kiss have not vanquished you, and since your incurably noble heart cannot be intoxicated by banal sensualities, I will speak. You are suffering, Stellus, because you are not similar to other men, because you cannot know their joys, nor their hopes, because you have obscure dreams within you, unnamed passions that you cannot express in words. But it is necessary that you know now that all men are, like you, solitary monsters.

"Do you remember, Stellus, when you were a small child, you could not distinguish he-goats from rams and ewes from she-goats. And when you heard bleating in the distanced, you said: 'It's the livestock moaning.' As the he-goat differs from the ram, one man differs from another. What is called humankind is only a disorderly flock of unknown and disparate beings.

"Stellus, the clairvoyant eyes of initiates perceive differences where vulgar eyes only see evident similarities. But men, ignoring the horrible, divine truth, believe themselves to be similar to one another. They speak to one another, the insensates, as if words could go from one soul to another. They look at one another as if they were not separated by insurmountable walls of darkness.

"You, Stellus, have understood obscurely that you are the only one of your race. It is for that reason, Stellus, that you have suffered. You appear to yourself to be different from other men, and you cannot resign yourself to your nobility. You fled into the forest because your companions were strangers to you, and you suffered in the forest because you no longer had companions. You loved solitude in the country because you suffered from being alone in crowds, and you have not been able to seek the deliverance promised by prophesies.

"Yes, the priests told the truth. You are of a noble race. But madly, like the others, you have searched for others of your race on earth. You have searched for them among soldiers and kings, and you thought you had found an equal when you had only encountered a lover. I have revealed secrets to you. Meditate, in order that you might one day, in accordance with what has been predicted, be delivered from the maleficent approaches of those you cannot believe to be your brothers."

Outside the gardens, outside the palace where his wife was asleep, Stellus drew away. He marched in stony plains; he climbed arid slopes; he followed the banks of funereal rivers. He came eventually into a land overhung by harsh mountains with sheer and smooth walls.

The inhabitants of the country that Stellus had entered were in affliction, because, from the heights of the mountains, a monstrous winged horse vomiting flames had fallen upon their houses. The hippogriff with diamond hooves shook the walls of the ancient houses with its resounding wings. It pawed the ground, tore up the sown grain, felled the oxen during the plowing; it abducted virgins, carrying them beyond the clouds. Then they were seen falling to earth, naked and bloody, like red and white flowers falling from the opening sky.

A great clamor had resounded at the advent of the monster, as imperious and loud as the voice of a herald, and prophetic words had been perceived. The victorious hippogriff would devastate the country until a man would voluntarily sit down between the scintillating wings and consent to go with the monster toward the stars.

Stellus arrived among those frightened people. He saw the monster from afar, and a hope rose up in his heart. Radiant, he went to find the village chiefs, and proclaimed that he would mount the hippogriff. The men saluted Stellus with long cries of admiration; the women embraced his knees and spread oils and balms over his feet.

The sages harangued the people. "See," they said, "the man who will sacrifice himself for you.

He is young and glorious; he could live royal years, and yet he will quit the soft dusts on which we walk with joy; he will leave the natal mud, in which we delight; he will go toward the foreign stars, toward the sky at which prudent men do not like to look. Glory to the hero! Contemplate the man who loves us enough to flee the earth, the man who will be devoured for his fellows."

While they spoke, Stellus, seizing the resplendent mane with both hands, intoned a song of delight: "Hippogriff, liberator hippogriff, carry me higher than the sky. In order to obey the divine old man, we shall go, O monster, beyond the gates of the horizon. I shall ride above cities, above landscapes where I have suffered. If nothing awaits us above the worlds, let us wander forever in the desert of the constellations. You will spring from the earth through the night of joyful stars, and I shall be delivered; I shall no longer have to endure human beings, I shall no longer have to love human beings and I shall finally know, freely, among the mute stars, the voluptuousness of being born solitary. But if I have merited, O savior monster, discovering those who are of my race, carry me toward them. Winged horse, charger worthy of a noble cavalier, carry me at last to where my true brethren are. Hippogriff, liberator hippogriff, like a king returning from a battle, I shall reenter the realm of life, toward my high celestial dwelling."

Stellus caressed the colored mane of the winged horse. The astral vaults opened peacefully to their course; the breezes of the heavens murmured words of welcome; luminous blonde forms leaned over on the clouds and, through the mists of a strange dawn, the solitary finally saw, burning in the utmost distance of the skies, the light for which he had searched so long, the light of fraternal eyes.

ARMENTARIA
(Sixth Century)

THAT EVENING, the spirit of the Lord visited the house and Armentaria died. She had languished since the summer, but that day the illness increased so rapidly that the young woman did not even have time to return to her apartment. She expired in the oratory while she was praying.

A maidservant who was waiting for her at the door—for she was a captive from Thuringia, still pagan—heard the body fall on to the paving-stones. Having entered, she saw Armentaria lying on the floor, supine, her arms outspread; and by the will of God, the light crucifix of sculpted wood before which the dying woman had been praying had fallen on to the breast of the corpse, piously.

There was a great tumult in the house. Servants, in all haste, went in search of Florentius, Armentaria's young husband; for he was absent that evening, having gone to assist a pauper who was dying. The servants came to the hut of the pauper and said: "Master! Master! Your wife is dead."

Florentius uttered a loud cry and fled toward his house.

Already the young women of the neighborhood had come running. They had carried Armentaria to her nuptial bed. Some searched the coffers for white garments to ornament the woman who would no longer ornament herself. Others went down into the gardens, which are sad and deflowered in that season in the land of Neustria, but a few precious flowers subsisted there, because virgins who were to be married before the spring kept them jealously for the morning of the wedding, and visited them amorously every day. However, without any regret, all the brides-to-be went to pick the last flowers for the funerary bed, for they loved the young woman who had died.

While they were honoring Armentaria thus, Florentius arrived.

"Go away, I beg you," he said, "in order that I might be alone with her."

Martial, the bishop, and Crescentius, a deacon, presented themselves. "The young women will go away, but we, as men of God, will remain in order to console you."

But Florentius sent the bishop and the deacon away too.

When everyone had left the house, Florentius, having sat down next to the bed, began to weep abundantly. He was not carried away by a tumultuous dolor, but he allowed his tears to flow, slow and almost peaceful. In the silence, however, his dolor was exalted, and as if his wife were able to hear him, he spoke to her.

"Dear virgin," he murmured amid his sobs, "dear virgin!" And he kissed the cold and pure hands that reposed in the midst of the flowers like sleeping doves. "Alas, alas, why have you deprived me of yourself? Why have you not been my wife? Everyone believed us to be mortal lovers, fortunate in sensual pleasure, while we lay side by side, and our lips were never united in a kiss. Sometimes, however . . . I remember . . . sometimes, your hand trembled in mine, did it not? But you purified the hand that had trembled with the sign of the cross, and we went to sleep side by side under the guard of the Lord. I have suffered, Armentaria; I have suffered a long passion by your gentle will, and no one knows our divine secret. And now they will bury you as a wife, you who ought to be saluted among the blessed virgins . . ."

Slowly, Florentius marched back and forth in the funereal chamber. The odor of flowers was heavy; the candles also charged the air with perfumes. Florentius opened the window overlooking the fields. Then he thought about the men who were down below in the mute houses. Perhaps, at that very moment, spouses were embracing one another, lovers sleeping together voluptuously.

Scattered in a mist of dream, he saw fortunate couples, and a mysterious pride fermented in his heart. Doubtless alone among all those men, he had been able to renounce permitted joys. He rejoiced; he sensed, rising within him, the intoxication of being a saint.

"I want them to know," he murmured. "I want them to know our secret."

Among the fading flowers, the dead woman sat up. Over her face, blanched a little while before, a blush spread, for it was an ineffable modesty that was revealing itself.

"Don't talk about that," she begged, extending her supernatural arms toward her husband. "Don't diminish our glory. I want you to be like me, my beloved. Don't talk about that. By your silence, you will merit long amorous conversations in heaven. Don't divulge anything, my Florentius. Virtue is only entire if it is secret. And it is still little if it is secret; it is worth more if it is denied. If I had wanted to be revered on earth as a virgin, could I not have lived in retreat with Radegonde?[1] A long time ago, Avitus, Bishop of Vienna, wanted to take me to the good queen. Do you know, my beloved, why I did not consent? It seemed to me that those virgins consecrated publicly to the Lord must take a secret pride in their merit. Men knew their virtue and praised it. For myself, I would have had a kind of divine shame in being chaste in the eyes of all. What offended my virginal modesty was that my virginity was known. It was for that reason, Florentius, that I wanted the pretended marriage. I wanted to pass for a life in order to be a virgin mysteriously. And now, I implore you, my Florentius, not to reveal our secret to those who will come. In order that our souls can be healthy, let us renounce all glory, especially that of being sanctified on earth. Let us be pure in the darkness and let us go to heaven silently."

Having sobbed for a long time, Florentius leaned over the woman who had gone back to sleep, and prayed to the Lord; and peace returned to his heart. The dawn—a soft, sad dawn—had risen; the morning wind extinguished the candles.

The bishop, the deacon and the pious women came to bury Armentaria.

---

1 The Frankish queen Radegonde (c520-587) was a princess of Thuringia who founded the Abbaye Sainte-Croix in Poitiers—which is still thriving—and became the patron saint of numerous other churches.

Then Martial, the bishop said: "Florentius, the serfs of the church, will take away Armentaria's body, but you know, as a Christian, that death is a brief and vain separation. You know that you will see your wife again. So, do not address long and desperate adieux to her. Embrace her as if she were departing for a short voyage, embrace her as you embrace her every morning as you quit her."

Meekly, Florentius approached the bed. He inclined before the bishop, and everyone heard him reply: "I will embrace my wife as I embraced her every morning."

And, shivering with his radiant lie, he approached his lips for the first time to the lips he had never brushed.

A PARTIAL LIST OF SNUGGLY BOOKS

www.ingramcontent.com/pod-product-compliance
Lightning Source LLC
Chambersburg PA
CBHW032043180726
48284CB00008B/2723